The Pregnant Mare

or

The Guys
in The Crate
at The Joint

Garrison Somers

art by Susan Connors

Published by **The Blotter Magazine**, Inc.
Text copyright 2016 by Garrison Somers
Illustrations copyright 2014 by Susan Connors

First Printing 2017

Published in the United States by
Lightfinger Books
an imprint of The Blotter Magazine, Inc.
1010 Hale Street, Durham, NC 27705

Printed and bound in the USA

"The Pregnant Mare"

by Garrison Somers

illustrated by Susan Connors

Dedicated to Ron and Michael,
who both believe that a good story
doesn't care who tells it.
-GS

The Crate was empty, they'd learned way back that a Texas April wasn't always predictable and shoveling newly soaking-wet manure was no picnic. 'Nother words, you carried what you needed when you needed it, no earlier. She squatted way out by the road's shoulder, drawing flies and making citizens swerve around while Rom and Ree ate lunch up on the porch. No one had told them to eat outside, but the two men had agreed a long time ago that for some people horse dung residue and store-bought lunch just don't mix. Better to eat out here, in the shade of a tin awning. The good old Dodge dumper with the two-by-six risers on the sides stank to high heaven no matter what Ree did: fully four of those green Christmas trees dangled from the rear-view mirror and he'd dropped an additional seven dollars at Wal-Mart on some sort of deodorizing device that filled with some kind of oil and reacted to heat which you could plug into the cigarette lighter that Rom kept carelessly yanking out whenever he needed to light his soggy Havatampa and so now you had to jiggle it every time the truck went over a bump and in their town there were a lot of bumps. Through a puff of some fairly nasty smoke, Rom concluded that buying the whole thing had been a waste of hard earned cash, because this was a manure truck and there was nothing you could do about that and stop trying, OK? One result of their line of work was that his personal sense of smell had been burnt out some-what, a little like a chandelier with some dark bulbs perched like fingers on its delicate gilt arms.

They kept their hair short and tucked beneath flat-caps, so you might be hard-pressed to guess their ages. Neither wore glasses, or walked with a cane, or silently suffered strangely painful complaints of the nether-regions. Maybe hard work keeps you from breaking before its time for you to be broke, Ree would tell you if you asked. Or it was pure-T *dumbluck*. Who could say? They had seen real things, too. It hadn't always been smooth sailing just out of sight. Their mom had given them truths: when they could talk and when they shouldn't even be there. You get a knack for staying in the shade, when the heat is high. Back in the day, young white boys would go looking for trouble, and a pair of black boys was perfect trouble. So when there was a chance to get out, even a war, they took it. Rom saw his elephant out in the Pacific as a cook and scullery able-bodied seaman:

once he had taken over as loader on a forty millimeter *ack-ack* against a Nip suicide flyer when the white gunner's mate had fallen down dead. And Ree had been with those Tuskegee airmen. Why not? When they were shirt-tail lads, he'd leaped from the shallow-pitched roof of their house - perhaps he'd been

talked into it by Rom, per- haps not. In any case, he'd been so close to flying before he came down and sprained his ankle that

he'd fallen in love then and there
with the idea of it. But he'd gone to
Alabama and then Italy and had gotten no closer than the near-magical
repair of the college boy's P-40
Warhawks. Once, when he beefed
about it, the squadron's commander
had told him personally he was far
too important keeping other pilots'
planes in the air to put into the air
himself. Which may or may not
have been a pail of manure, but it
didn't much matter - he got no flight
time at all. So even though he once
had actually shaken hands with ol'
Mrs. Roosevelt he didn't lord anything over his brother. Coming
home *alive in '45*, both of them had
to admit that they'd seen more than

enough of the wide world. At the same time, they knew they'd been lucky, for the wide world hadn't troubled them much. Now they were in their - lord, who can say how old? - healthy and still working.

And they *were* brothers; the real deal and not that thing that those hippity-hoppers called brothers which just meant some fool you're hanging around with and getting drunk with and letting steal your money. Brothers and friends from birth. Momma had passed quite a few years back and Daddy'd been gone for so long they never talked about him at all. Certainly he was dust now and had been such a measly iota of a nothing in their minds that verification of such an event wouldn't have mattered. Neither Rom nor Ree had ever gotten married, although the idea had occurred to them of course and there had been a few women who had placed themselves in their path for such a purpose. Time was when they might have attributed this lack to thinking on Daddy's behaviors, but that was so long ago it didn't matter anymore. Now when they thought about the arrival of spring and birds and bees, it was mostly all the gardens out there in the world and how they all needed compost and so when Ree said to Rom, "What kind of candy you want ol' Easter Bun' to bring you?" Rom was joshing when he said it, winking as he always did, "Eye candy, 'course."

Another truth: they had each other and that was sufficient and it was quite something that so much water had passed under the bridge and still they preferred each other's company to alone, choosing to live just outside of town in a neat shotgun shack, painted a shade of blue that had resulted from mixing a gift of six partial-gallons a customer had given to get the cans out of their garage. Once, maybe, this might have meant that they were poor, but the town had chosen to grow rather than dissipate – the only two directions for towns to take – and developers of such things had found their acres valuable and so they had sold some of them. Nobody but the man at the bank knew that the brothers were comfortable. Not rich – that term had taken on a whole new meaning in the years intervening from the war until now – but they had a steady investment income which covered their needs. What they made working was pocket money, and they didn't go crazy and all, and they were fairly happy with those things they already had.

Like, for example, driving around that nasty old truck which used to have a girl's name, but now they just called The Crate. Hey, Rom might say if the subject came up, it wasn't The Crate's fault that she'd gone and lost her name. Supposing you carry around horse manure for so long, which despite its benefits for your tomahts and pickling-cukes has its *rude-amentory* as well as *old-factory* hazards inasmuch as you can't travel down a highway or byway lest some citizen comes up behind you waving their hand in front of their face and rolling up their windows on even the hottest summer day and then finally passing you with a long honk on the tooter and a burst of smoky exhaust.

Now you know folks're thinking *there's those fool colored men and that damned crate of theirs, stinking up the place, for crying out loud.* More truth: the truck had become such a part of them that their fannies conformed to the spots on the bench-seat so perfectly that Ree was now always the driver with Rom riding permanent shotgun. And even though Momma had named them Romulus and Remus – two tough little fellas raised by wolves to found the whole by-god Roman Empire – by the time LBJ was president as far as folks in town were concerned the brothers were just 'those colored men who drive that crate of a manure truck'. Outnumbered and surrounded, so to speak, Rom and Ree surrendered like Joe Johnston's Rebs in Durham and the old truck with its once-upon-a-time affectionate girl's name became The Crate and wasn't that how things always went and who was hurt by it, anyway?

So they had each other and regular work and a little bit of fun, because in the fullness of time you learned where things come from and where things go and how much you can afford to pay for that which aint free and how much to charge others for things you yourself got for free.

"It's a science, business is, but what you might call a soft science," Ree said, apparently out of the blue, but in fact apropos of some conversation they'd been having off and on for a while. They sat on smooth-seated wooden benches on the rough cut plank porch in front of the Joint, having consumed double-meat cheeseburgers all the way, which meant with sweet grilled onions, lettuce, *tomaht*, and just a wee dash of Tabasco. (They'd been ordering these same burger sandwiches since when the rules were the rules and the porch was as far as they were allowed to go. There was a long ago nailed shut little window around on the kitchen side where colored folks as wanted to could place an order back in the day.) Ree sipped at a bottle of Orange Crush and Rom was smoking his ever-present cigar, somehow drawing in the smoke while chewing around the wet end of the rolled tobacco leaf in a way that Ree found fascinating and also a little bit disgusting.

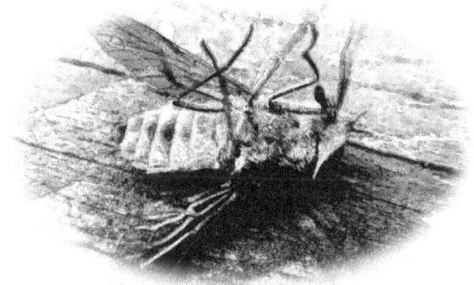

"Say that more'n half of all new businesses go bust in the first year?" Rom posed rhetorically to his brother. They'd been talking about such thing since learning that the fellow who owned the Joint and worked galley-slave hours at the grill,

was thinking about retiring and sell-
ing the place, lock, stock and burger-
recipe. Ree nodded and took another sip. "Gotta get your *model* right,
for return on investment and for
managing your cash."

"That's where most folks go
wrong. Can't meet payroll, you're
done. They got no idea that it's all
about cash, after all," Rom frowned.

"Not surprising," Ree spoke soft-
ly. "They ought to call it uncom-
mon sense. People are crazy most of
the time. Do fool things. Don't do
business with someone on account
of color or belief or who they choose
to love or some other thing. Like
the world's not already too competi-
tive to tell customers to go away. Or

they're just silly, buying themselves a pretty chair and desk for a new comp'ny aint even made a dime." He knew that Rom had heard all of his opinions on basic business management before, but greatly enjoyed chatting after a meal. And no one down in the capital was ever going to invite Rom and Ree to talk in front of a gymnasium full of shiny faces, but that would be their loss. There was university learning, and practical learning, and a man might find it was good to have both in their measure. Success came along in recognizing when to use one or the other.

"Like what?" Rom asked. "I mean you're right and all. But how do you mean people do fool things in business particular?" He liked sitting quietly, alternately chewing or puffing on his corona, while the dust stirred up a little from all Ree's talking.

"I mean goin' to business in the first place, said Ree. "We need more clothes-selling stores, or furniture places where you got to paint the furniture yourself, or TV repair shops after it's less 'spensive to buy a new TV than pay to fix it like we need a new hole in our head. But out there you got folks who're thinking 'I got me an idea with money written all over it.' You know, a man has got to come up with better plans before he spends any money on a cell telephone and cards with his name on them." Ree scratched his chin, where a thatch of curly hair grew. He had more to say about it, like banks and bankruptcy laws and suchlike, but it was time to stop preaching. His brother had finished his burger and was wiping his face with an old handkerchief, ragged but clean white. The cigar still refused to budge, so he wiped around it with precision. Rom didn't care so much about the why's of things, anyway, even though he himself had asked the question.

"They lie," Rom said with conviction, thinking generally about some Chief Financial Officers, all elected officials and any baseball players who'd ever been on drugs. He puffed on the corona, but it had gone out during the munching of his cheeseburger.

"Some of 'em cheat," Ree added, recognizing instantly the tack that his brother was taking with the conversation and thinking about telephone salesmen, college football coaches and used car dealers. He tipped his soda bottle to wash down his last bite of burger.

"How'd you get so smart?" Rom asked with a grin.

"Just naturally brilliant, I guess," Ree smiled with his eyes closed under the mid-day glare of post-rain spring sunshine. Comfortable, it was.

One blessed thing about working

for yourself was that you made your own hours. Ree and Rom occasionally scheduled work, but not often. There had been that time when they had to clean up after an...accident at this woman's house. Seemed that there'd been a long, drawn, drag-out fight between the town's two long-ago-graduated majorettes, a feud simmering and festering over the years. One thing had led as it will to another and the result was a honey-wagon full of cockroaches dumped in the front door of one of the women's homes. Lord, she'd gone a bit crazy, stalking down the street to get revenge, armed with her twirling-irons, planning to thump the other woman into submission. Only because she'd been caught by the night-shift policeman in the hood-lamp of his prowler, she'd not brought insult to injury. He'd made her walk slowly home, steam fairly rising from her anger, in what was now referred to throughout the town as *The Baton Death March*. When she finally called them on the phone to come clean up her foy-ay, it was two in the morning. Her voice was so...stressed, they'd scheduled her right in and pulled on their coveralls and galoshes.

The two men cleared their table, so to speak, pitching their wrappers and empties into the trash bin by the old gasoline pump, an antique that hadn't spilt a drop of mid-range

octane since the oil *embar-no-go* of 'seventy-four. The Joint had taken over the empty Sinclair station, brought in a grill, tables, chairs, fridges, candy racks and a lottery machine and started making burgers from an old family recipe that entailed, among other things, using a eight ounce bottle of Coke to flatten the patties. Soon it was known far and wide for its fare and was turning a land-office business. The colored men ate lunch there every day, always outside.

"Look at that over there," Ree said to no one in particular. Rom had heard this preface before, many times.

"Yeah," Rom said anyway, because that is what brothers do.

"That gas pump's exactly what I mean. How you manage to go out of business pumping gas?" Ree shook his head in wonder. "In Tex-by-god-Ass."

"Your mouth," his brother said with a deep frown. "Come on, now."

Ree raised his eyebrows in lieu of

an apology.

"I'm just saying."

"Sometimes you sound like that hip-hop." Rom said. "Your language."

"Said I was sorry," Ree replied, although he hadn't, actually.

"And what kind of memories you think you have in your old age when your music aint carrying a tune in a pail and then it's all about cursing, fighting, and chasing tail? No wonder..." Rom shook his head, cutting himself short because he'd moaned and groaned about the shortcomings of modern popular music before. Ree countered that with an affirmative nod, although he wasn't sure at this moment what there was not to wonder. He couldn't imagine that his brother was worried about his old-age memories, and let it go at that.

They sat down again, to let their food settle.

"Bikram Yoga." Ree finally said after enough moments that anyone else listening in might have imagined that the old man had fallen asleep on his bench and had awakened from a dream with two strange words fluttering around in his skull.

"What's that?" Rom asked, slightly surprised to hear new and different words coming out of his brother's mouth.

"Up and coming business, if you want to know. Exercising in a hot room. I swear. All kinds of women do it. Some men, too. Say it's good for you. You actually pay to go." Ree had read about this in a women's magazine. Redbook, maybe, or Cosmo, he didn't quite remember.

"That so?" Mildly interesting.

"Bet there's not one in town."

"Bet there's not one in Texas. Already hot in Texas. Coals to Newcastle," Rom sniffed.

There was no longer a cloud in the sky, but the two men didn't say a thing about it. Some things - the beauty of a single day - needed no shared words. That morning had included a load dropped for Doctor Kenny, who had a painless-dentist office in town next to the menswear store. Rom and Ree had gone to his home. They hadn't asked, assuming he'd take an extra couple of buckets'-worth on his own to spread in his office window-boxes. The brothers took care not to drive downtown any more than necessary, which was fortunately not too often. They were also mindful how they dumped their load on his driveway, shoveling out the bed of the truck onto a deep-barrow and then tipping that carefully onto the same spot as last year and the year before.

"Ol' Doctor Kenny uses gloves," Ree said.

"He does, indeed. Yeah, well,

they make you do that now," Rom said, finally shifting his well-teethed cigar over to the other side.

"For spreading horseshit on his oleanders is what I meant," Ree chuckled.

"I can understand that," his brother replied. "I don't particularly want my own hands in my mouth much." He smiled broadly around his cigar. He was proud of his teeth. He had but one missing, where a tiny piece of shrapnel from an exploding *Zeke* had whickered through the air and nipped at his face. He'd been a twenty-millimeter loader, which meant hard lifting work. His mouth had been open, panting from thirst from the longevity of this particular *battle-stations*, and the red-hot tid-bit of metal had touched his gum in front, cutting the root of a tooth, and continued on its way without troubling anything else. He'd hardly noticed its passing, other than the salty blood which he had stanched with a piece of gauze. But his tooth had died, turning first gray and then black. A Navy dentist had removed it and left the hole. Later, when he could afford it, Rom had it replaced with an enamel double, fastened perfectly to its partners on the left and right. After all these years, only fingernails, hair and a tooth lost. Not bad, if you consider the possibilities.

It was time for them to return to

work, but they kept their seats. At
that moment a small blue four-door
Nissan, pulled up. A man, a
woman, and two young boys climbed
from the car. They were rumpled
and unsteady. The man was tall but
bent, rubbing the small of his back
with his palms, and the woman was
prim and vaguely pretty, small-
boned. Standing, she tied a kerchief
around her hair to keep it out of the
sun.

"Long drive," Ree said quietly to
Rom.

The man raised his sunglasses to
peer at The Joint.

"Well, I'm hungry," he said in a
too-loud voice, as if the noise within
the car had been fierce and he could-

n't yet hear himself think.

"Honey, it doesn't seem quite clean," said the woman, apparently his wife. "Let's keep going until we see a McDonalds"

"Yeah, Dad. McDonalds," said the taller of the two boys, whose face was both pudgy and pinched-looking, like he was battling something sour in his stomach.

"Pleeeeze!" squalled son number two. "I don't want dirty food."

"He's going to get back in that car, you watch," said Rom under his breath. "Miss a good meal, maybe a chili-frito-pie and a cold drink, on account of he's too tired to tell her no."

"She's tired, too," said Ree, not

taking her side but just observing aloud.

"Yeah, but it's just a physical tired. He...he's got that mental tired can't be helped. It's called *metaphysical*. Some folks reach a point in their life where they don't have the energy to disagree anymore. It don't

matter what about – politics, phone bill, their wife, the Lord God. They just say *Yeah, OK*, and they shuffle on through the rest."

"He's married, though. Marriage is a covenant based on trust. He made a decision; he needs to explain to her why he made it, listen to her side, and if her argument's unsound, he's gotta stick with it," Ree said. "Until death does he part." He tee-heed behind his curled hand, pretending he was coughing, adjusted his flat-cap.

The husband was still standing there, staring under his sunglasses. For a long moment, he seemed turned to stone.

"No, I want to eat here," he said

in a flat tone.

"Hang on. Mister Man's making a stand," whispered Rom. "Doing it all wrong, but still. He should of said 'we eating here' instead, but we'll forgive him because it's probably his first stand."

"Oooh. This aint the hill he want to die on, though," said Ree. "Watch ol' wife now. Angry. Pretty woman, but her face is all stove up, like she gotta go bad." He sucked on the tailings in the bottle of Orange Crush.

"I'm not sure I can eat here. If you don't want McDonalds we can keep looking. This looks like it was an old gas station. How clean do you think it could be? God, all of that grease and gasoline and..." the wife spurted all in one breath before petering out. Her own voice was up a notch, like she was struggling not to snipe at him. She tossed off one more thought for good measure. "You know, they fake their board of health ratings."

"Yeah, they fake their border help ratings," mis-repeated the younger son. "I want McDonalds."

"I bet you on a long drive, they want to pitch that child out on the road from time to time," said Ree. "Without even dee-celerating."

"No doubt," said Rom, biting back a grin.

The man still hadn't surrendered. He stepped towards the front door, then stopped, as if he had felt pressure against his chest, or his wife had a long, strong elastic band wrapped around him back to herself, wrangling him into submission. He seemed to shrink, as if his backbone was collapsing like dominoes.

"Let's get back in the car," he told his wife. She had started to cross her arms and stopped in mid-cross.

"Go inside and ask where the nearest McDonalds is," she said.

"Oh, boy, here it comes," Rom said. "Caving in like an old copper mine."

The husband turned deliberately, his eyebrows furrowing like a rut in the middle of his forehead.

"You can't go into a burger place and ask where a different burger place is," he said. He rubbed the flat of his hand through his hair, as defiantly as he dared.

"Of course you can," she said, matter-of-factly.

"It just isn't done." But he was deflating rapidly against the practiced wall of *her*.

"What are you talking about?" she replied in lilting tones.

He inhaled deeply and exhaled, loud enough for the two men on the porch to hear him.

He knew that she had won.

"Yeah, Dad..." said the older son, but he was cut off by his father with a glare so withering that it took six months off his life without either of them knowing it at the time. It was a *you'll see* look. The son would remember that terrible look most intimately when he was in his mid-sixties and beginning to display the early-onset symptoms of Alzheimer's Syndrome. The withering look would frequently enter his nightmares, causing him to evacuate his bowels loosely into his pajamas in the middle of the night so often that his own long-suffering wife finally had him committed to an advanced-care facility in North Lauderdale, Florida, and after a while stopped visiting.

"Good one," said Rom. Ree was chuckling so hard that he was forced to camouflage it by blowing his nose into his handkerchief with a loud honk that inadvertently turned the family's attention to the two colored men sitting on the porch.

The wife's stare oozed such a phenomenal heap of scorn that Ree flinched and mumbled "Damn" and Rom bit down on a new Havatampa he'd just unwrapped, scoring it and damaging all future potential for its drawing smoke. She aimed back at her husband, forcing him to lift each foot and walk towards the door to The Joint.

"Time to go," Rom said and he stood. Ree pitched his empty Orange Crush bottle in the recycle can with a clatter and followed his brother. They should have stayed put, and quiet. Husband might have ignored two elderly colored gentlemen sitting on the front porch, choosing rather to inquire directions of the lady at the cash register, possibly purchasing a couple of scratch and play lottery tickets as cover for the vastness of his embarrassment and the insult of being too fine a person to have a Joint burger. But two men moving innocuously towards him in the parking lot he could not allow to escape unqueried.

"McDonalds?" he said, eyebrows risen in an unspoken 'can you please release me from this ridiculous situation?'

Now, in their long, full lives Rom

and Ree had experienced the best and worst that Texas could offer in terms of Jim Crow, and after all of that monkey-business they had to admit that white people could be good folks or ugly bastards. Old Lyndon Baines himself was a prime example of both factors residing if

PLEASE CLEAN UP AFTER HORSES

not too uncomfortably at least uni-
formly in the same flesh. Most of
the time, however, you never knew
what you were up against. They'd
made it a long-standing habit to just
avoid confrontations with the paler
of the species. Living to Ripe Old
Age and To-Tell-The-Tale was reward
in itself. But there were times, like
today, that being black and old in
the South was pure pleasure. The
two brothers had seen the Illinois
license plate on the man's Nissan.

"McDonalds?" Rom repeated, as
if he were hard of hearing, or as sim-
pleminded as Husband imagined,
either one being just fine. He
stopped still and peered out from
under his flat cap and around his

broken cigar. Ree, walking bent all crooked-like, peeked around his brother.

"What?" Ree said, loudly.

"Man here say 'McDonalds'," Rom turned his whole body, like his ancient neck was as stiff as old yard-hose, to face Ree.

"No. This aint McDonalds, you old fool!" Ree bawled at his brother.

"I know that!" Rom bawled back. "Quit yelling at me!"

"No, no. I mean, do you know where the closest McDonalds is?" asked Husband, holding his arms out and wondering what manner of Pandora's Box he had opened by speaking to these two men. *Oh, God, stop shouting.*

Rom turned back, without bending his neck, or even his knees now, a robot with stiff joints. He acknowledged the question with a frown and turned creakingly back to Ree.

"Oh! Man wants to know where McDonalds is."

"Burger place?" Ree asked.

"Yeah," said Rom, patiently.

"Got a burger place right here." Ree lifted his hand towards the sky, as if revealing a universal truth. He then bit his own tongue hard to stifle a rise of the giggles.

Rom turned back slowly towards Husband.

"He right about that. They's burger place right here. Good burger place, called Joint." Rom pointed all bent-fingered up at the hand-painted sign over the awning where they had been sitting as if he was Diogenes suddenly coming upon an honest man.

"Best burgers around," Ree added.

"Ahem," said Husband. He seemed willing to discuss it further, having suddenly added two people to his side of the argument. Wife, however, had arrived, her heels kicking up sparks on the gravel. You could smell the stink of frustration in her breath and sweat and her very pheromones acting as a repulsion agent expelled in an aura around her. Everyone stepped back.

"Honey, did you ask where the closest McDonalds is?" she said, dripping venom, knowing that he had already.

"Oh, McDonalds! They's one of them in Tyler," Ree said, seemingly recovered from his dementia. "They's another in Nacogdoches."

"You talkin' Natchadoches," Rom said.

"No, that's in Loo-she-anna. I mean Nacogdoches, down the interstate a way to Houston," Ree clarified, pronouncing both quite-different cities' names precisely the same.

They watched without moving facial muscle, almost without breathing. Husband was suddenly relaxing. The pressure was off him. There was no point getting angry with a couple of loony old men arguing in what seemed a strange multi-syllabic language. It couldn't be helped. He looked at Wife and she had grown quite pink now, ostensibly on her way to angry red. He actually felt the faint beginning of a warm happy glow in his belly at such a development.

"Which one is the closest?" Husband asked Rom, almost leaning over as if he were talking to a child.

"Closest," repeated Rom, thinking aloud, or perhaps suffering from echolalia. He resisted scratching the top of his hat because it would have been too silly, even for this. He turned and cocked his head, deferring to Ree.

Ree looked up and down the air-port road. He had no idea where the closest McDonalds was nor did he really care. They had a load to pick up at Cokesbury's farm and it was a hand-load, which meant using nothing but shovels. You see, Cokesbury had a pregnant mare and she didn't like too much ruckus, so said shoveling would take a good part of the afternoon. They should-n't waste any more time on this fool-ishment. Still, just to add a tad more insult to injury, Ree looked up in the sky, as if that were a burger-directional option for the Illinois family, or that he was receiving instructions from the Almighty.

Small clouds scudded overhead, but there was no more rain in the forecast. He and Rom could work through dinner if they had to. Weighing his next words carefully he looked Wife in the eye.

"Oh, it just 'long the road a piece. Two lights first, then turn right and maybe two minutes. Right where the road fork, keep an eye out for it. Over old fishing bridge and there you go. Can't miss." He waved his finger around randomly with each direction change. Aw, they wouldn't get lost, but if they could follow his words, they'd end up at a local place that served some damn fine Tex-Mex chow. If Husband had any cojones, they would eat there and be the better for it. Actually, if Husband really had some, he'd eat there alone, and leave the brats and Wife out sitting in the car.

"Thank you," Wife clipped, and she headed back for the Nissan. Husband dipped his head in thanks to the colored gentlemen and took the two boys by the hand. At that moment, as it is oft wont to do in East Texas, the wind picked up - an invisible swirl of breeze that lifted a top layer of fine dust from the bed of the manure truck and draped it over the Nissan just as Wife was getting in the passenger's side.

"My! God!" she exclaimed, gagging. "What in the *Hell* was *that*?"

The horse-dung-dust missed Husband and boys, but Rom and Ree knew what had happened. Ol' God had come through for them again. They suppressed their grins mightily. Nothing personal about it. Just business.

They climbed into The Crate. Rom drove, quietly humming *Birdland*.

Susan Connors is an artist and animal lover in North Lauderdale, FL.

Garrison Somers is editor of The Blotter and Corner Bar Magazines in Durham, NC.
Lightfinger Books (an imprint of The Blotter Magazine, Inc.) *books* are intended for use by folks sitting in waiting rooms of hospitals. We believe that these readers would prefer not to be where they are. Often, there isn't much to do to pass the time and, maybe for just a moment, take one's mind off of those things that concern them most. We hope that these books help just a little bit with that very thing. If you would like to make a small donation to help offset printing costs of this and other Lightfinger Books, check us out on *www.blotterrag.com*.

We hope you enjoyed reading yet another
micro-novel brought to you by
Lightfinger Books
Collect 'em all & share with your friends.
For more information, to see our other shenanigans,
or to make a donation to our cause,
visit us at
www.blotterrag..com

www.ingramcontent.com/pod-product-compliance
Lightning Source LLC
Chambersburg PA
CBHW070650130626
46555CB00006B/2794